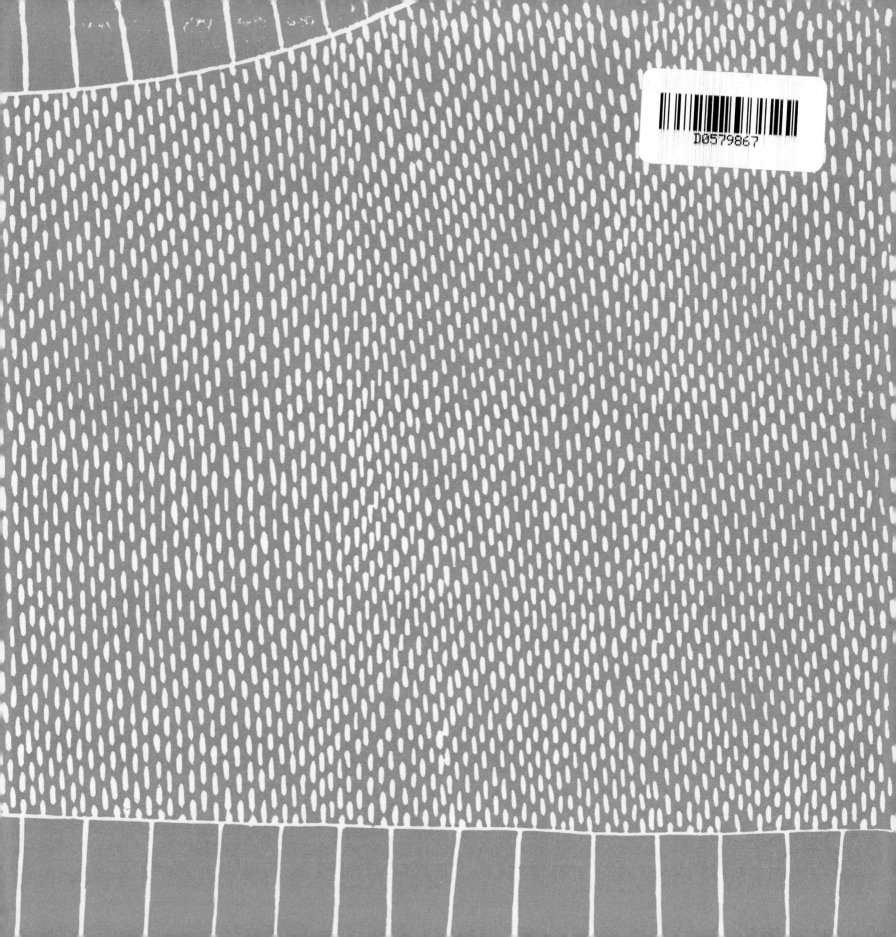

FOR MY NEPHEW YLFINGUR
XX

Library of Congress Cataloging-in-Publication Data
Names: Hood, Morag (illustrator), author, illustrator.
Title: Brenda is a sheep / Morag Hood.
Description: First American edition. | New York : Random House Children's Books, [2020]
"Originally published in a slightly different form by Two Hoots, an imprint of
Pan Macmillan, London, in 2019." | Audience: Ages 3–7. | Audience: Grades K–1.
Summary: "This story is a twist on the classic story of a wolf in sheep's clothing. Brenda, a wolf, is preparing a great
sheep feast, but the sheep have a different menu up their woolly sleeves." —Provided by publisher.
Identifiers: LCCN 2019031792 (print) | LCCN 2019031793 (ebook)
ISBN 978-0-593-17380-0 (hardcover) | ISBN 978-0-593-17381-7 (ebook)
Subjects: CYAC: Sheep—Fiction. | Wolves—Fiction. | Friendship—Fiction. | Humorous stories.
Classification: LCC PZ7.1.H655 Bre 2020 (print) | LCC PZ7.1.H655 (ebook) | DDC [E]—dc23

MANUFACTURED IN CHINA
10 9 8 7 6 5 4 3 2 1
First American Edition

MORAG HOOD

BRENDA IS A SHEEP

Random House · New York

These are sheep.

This is also a sheep.

This sheep is called Brenda.

Brenda has a very nice woolly sweater.

Brenda does all the
things that sheep do . . .

...because Brenda is a sheep.

The sheep learn lots of new games
from their friend Brenda.

Like catch,

teeth sharpening,

and tag. Brenda loves tag.

But no matter how hard she tries...

...she can never catch anyone.
They always get away.

The sheep think Brenda is probably
the best sheep they have ever met.

She is so very tall, she has nice pointy teeth,
and her wool is knitted and colorful.

All the sheep want to be just like Brenda.

BRENDA

But Brenda
has other things
on her mind.

She is working hard
on her special
mint sauce recipe.

The sheep have never had Brenda's special mint sauce, but she tells them it is very tasty.

You just need to find the right thing to eat it with.

Luckily, Brenda knows just
the thing. She is getting
ready for a feast.

The sheep are
very excited.

Brenda tells the sheep to go to bed nice and early. She says there will be a surprise for them in the morning.

A delicious surprise.

Brenda has to wait a very long time
for the sheep to go to sleep.

But at last they begin to nod off, one by one.
Brenda counts them on her claws.

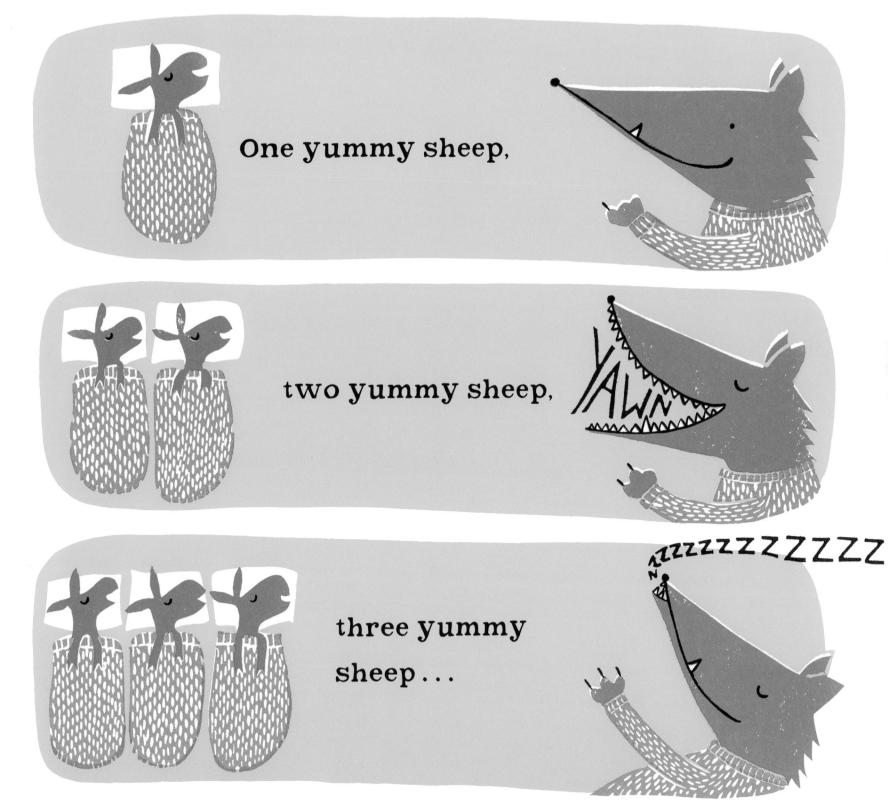

One yummy sheep,

two yummy sheep, YAWN

three yummy sheep . . .

ZZZZZZZZZZZ

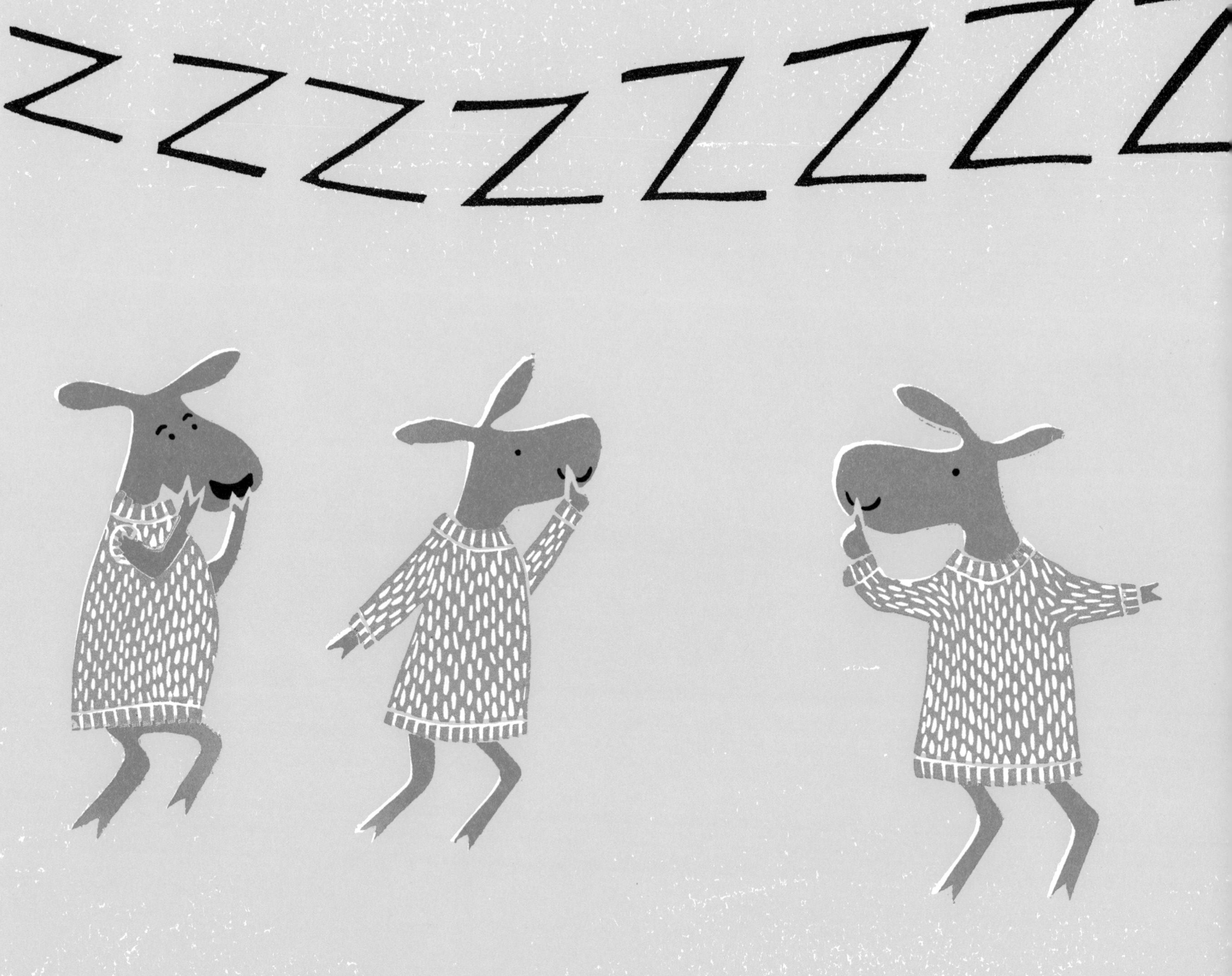
ZZZZZZZZ

BAAAA!

By the time Brenda wakes up, the sheep
have made a surprise of their own.

There is
grass stew

and grass
pie

and grass
burgers

and grass
lasagna

and grass
sandwiches

and grass
sausages.

And for dessert,
grass cookies.

With a delicious
sauce to pour
over it all.

This is not the feast Brenda had planned.